LITTLE MISS STUBBORN
the wrong advice

Original concept b
Illustrated and writter

MR.MEN   **LITTLE MISS**

MR. MEN and LITTLE MISS™ & © THOIP (a Chorion Company)

Printed and published under licence from Price Stern Sloan, Inc., Los Angeles.
Published in Great Britain by Egmont UK Limited
239 Kensington High Street, London W8 6SA
Printed in Italy. All rights reserved.
www.mrmen.com

EGMONT

How stubborn is Little Miss Stubborn?

I'll tell you.

She was driving along the other day when she came to a sign which said, 'BRIDGE WASHED AWAY!'

"Nonsense!" she cried. "If I want to drive along this road then I will!"

And she carried straight on ...

... into the river!

SPLASH!

Well, she would, wouldn't she?
There was no bridge.

That's how stubborn Little Miss Stubborn is.

The one thing she hates more than anything else in life is advice.

If you are as stubborn as Little Miss Stubborn, advice is there to be ignored.

For instance, she always walks under ladders.

She never wears a hat when it's cold.

And she always opens umbrellas indoors.

Not because she particularly wants to, but because she has been told that she shouldn't.

And needless to say, Little Miss Stubborn was fed up.

However, last Monday she met Little Miss Sunshine.

Miss Stubborn was covered in wet paint. The sign on the bench had read 'WET PAINT', but she had sat on the bench all the same.

"Do you know what your problem is?" said Miss Sunshine. "You always ignore good advice. You ought to start listening to what people have to say, and save yourself a lot of trouble."

On the way home Miss Stubborn thought about what Miss Sunshine had said.

And she thought about it over dinner.

And she stayed up all night thinking about it.

And by the morning she had decided that she would take Little Miss Sunshine's advice, which meant listening to everyone else's advice as well!

She set off into town, shopping.

The first person she met was Mr Wrong.

"Don't turn right at the end of the road, there's a hole in the ground," advised Mr Wrong.

Miss Stubborn was about to say, "Don't be ridiculous," when she stopped and remembered what she had decided.

"Thank you," she said.

When she got to the end of the road she turned left and ...

... fell down a hole!

BUMP!

Mr Wrong had got it wrong as usual.

The next day she took Little Miss Dotty's advice and used the hairdresser she recommended.

Oh dear!

She took Mr Silly's advice on the best place to buy an umbrella.

She took Little Miss Scatterbrain's advice on directions to the beach.

And Mr Dizzy told her about his new short-cut to avoid the traffic.

Little Miss Stubborn was fed up.

Again.

At the end of the week she met Little Miss Sunshine in the grocer's.

"Mind the ..." began Little Miss Sunshine.

"Stop," said Little Miss Stubborn. "No more advice."

"But ..."

"No!" said Little Miss Stubborn.

"You're about to ..."

"Not another word!" demanded Little Miss Stubborn, and turned and ...

... pointed to a sign.

"I know this is a slippery floor, but I want to go this way and so I will." And with that she slipped over.

BUMP!

"You really are the most stubborn person I know," laughed Miss Sunshine.

"No I'm not!"